STEP INTO READING®

MARC BROWN

ARTHUR LOSES A FRIEND

Random House New York

Published in the United States by Random House Children's Books, a division of Random House, Inc., New York.

www.stepintoreading.com

Educators and librarians, for a variety of teaching tools, visit us at
www.randomhouse.com/teachers

Library of Congress Cataloging-in-Publication Data
Brown, Marc Tolon.
Arthur loses a friend / Marc Brown. — 1st ed.
p. cm. — (Step into reading. Step 3)
SUMMARY: Buster goes away for a month, and Arthur becomes sad and confused
when he does not receive even one postcard from him.
ISBN-10: 0-375-82974-1 (trade) — ISBN-10: 0-375-92974-6 (lib. bdg.)
ISBN-13: 978-0-375-82974-1 (trade) — ISBN-13: 978-0-375-92974-8 (lib. bdg.)
[1. Friendship—Fiction. 2. Postcards—Fiction. 3. Aardvark—Fiction. 4. Rabbits—Fiction.]
I. Title. II. Series: Step into reading. Step 3 book.
PZ7.B81618Aldu 2006 [E]—dc22 2005008335

Printed in the United States of America 10 9 8 7 6 5 4 3 2 1 First Edition

Today was the last day
of school for Buster.
Tomorrow he was going
to his dad's for a month.

"Have fun, Buster,"

said Mr. Ratburn.

"But don't forget your homework."

Arthur went to the airport
to see Buster off.
"It's going to be great
to spend a whole month
with my dad," said Buster.

"I'll miss you," said Arthur.

"Don't worry," said Buster.

"I'll send lots of postcards."

Then he waved good-bye

and got on the plane.

The next day,

Arthur ran home from school.

"Any mail from Buster?"

he asked his mom.

"No," she said.

"He just left yesterday,"
said D.W.

Every day, Arthur looked
in the mailbox.
But there was nothing
from Buster.

Two weeks passed
and still not a word.
"Maybe Buster broke his arm
and can't write," thought Arthur.

Arthur called Buster's mom.
"How is Buster?"
he asked her.
"He's having so much fun,"
she said.
"He's been to a Red Sox game,
and he caught a big fish
on his dad's sailboat.

He's even made some friends.
He plays football with them."
"Oh," said Arthur.
"He writes me all about it
in his letters and postcards,"
said Buster's mom.

That night, Arthur said,
"I think Buster has forgotten
all about me."
"Have you written to him?"
Arthur's dad asked.

Arthur got a pen and paper.

He wrote:

Dear Buster,

Why haven't you written to me?

Your friend,

Arthur

The next day at school,
Arthur said to Francine,
"I just sent Buster a letter."
"I just got a letter from him,"
she said. "He's having fun."

"Buster's having so much fun,"
said Arthur to the Brain.
"Sounds like he has forgotten us."
The Brain held up a postcard.
"He didn't forget me,"
said the Brain.

Days passed.
At the dinner table,
Arthur played with his peas.
He didn't even finish
his bowl of strawberries.

"Can you believe it?" he said.
"Everyone has heard
from Buster but me."
"Don't worry," said his mom.
"You'll see him in two days."

"Don't be sad, Arthur,"
said D.W.
"You've got lots of friends."
"But Buster was my best friend,"
he said.

Arthur hugged Pal.
"You're my best friend now,"
he said. "But I wish
you could tell funny jokes
like Buster."

The next day, the mailman
called to Arthur,
"I have a lot of mail for you."
And he pulled out of his sack
ten postcards and three letters.

"Mrs. Hammer brought them
to the post office this morning,"
said the mailman. "She said,
'Stop bringing me these.
There is no Arthur
at 265 Main Street,
where I live.'
But I knew that there IS an Arthur
at 562 Main Street."

Arthur read Buster's postcards
and letters over and over.

"I'm having lots of fun,
but I really miss you,"
wrote Buster.
"This month with my dad
was really great,
but it will be great
to come home, too,"
he wrote in another letter.

Buster called Arthur
as soon as he got home.
"Can I come over?" he asked.
Arthur laughed.
"Sure, if you can find my house!"